Copyright © 1993 by Nord-Süd Verlag AG, Gossau Zürich, Switzerland
First published in Switzerland under the title *Nikis Eselchen*
English translation copyright © 1993 by North-South Books Inc., New York.

First published in the United States, Great Britain, Canada, Australia, and New Zealand
in 1993 by North-South Books, an imprint of Nord-Süd Verlag AG,
Gossau Zürich, Switzerland.

Distributed in the United States by North-South Books Inc., New York.

Library of Congress Cataloging-in-Publication Data is available
ISBN 1-55858-183-9 (trade binding)
ISBN 1-55858-184-7 (library binding)

British Library Cataloguing in Publication Data
Hol, Coby
Niki's Litle Donkey
I. Title II. James, J. Alison
823.914
ISBN 1-55858-183-9

10 9 8 7 6 5 4 3 2 1
Printed in Belgium

Niki's Little Donkey

By Coby Hol

Translated by J. Alison James

North-South Books / New York

Niki lived with her mother, her father, and her grandmother in a white house in the middle of a village on an island in Greece.

Niki's grandmother's name was Maria. All the villagers were fond of her and came to her when they needed advice. Because she was so wise, they all called her Yaiya, which means grandmother.

Niki's parents farmed a small piece of land just outside the village. There they had a field of vegetables and a stable for their two donkeys. Every day they pulled up the weeds between the plants and harvested tomatoes, peppers, cucumbers, and melons. Once a week everything had to be packed up in crates to be taken to the big market in town.

One day Niki had important news. She ran out to the field and called excitedly, "Baba, Mama, come quickly! The donkey had her baby!

"Isn't he sweet?" whispered Niki. She was so thrilled that she hopped from one foot to the other.

"He certainly is," Yaiya Maria said, smiling.

Niki turned to her father. "The donkey is so little, Baba! I can't wait to see him grow up so I can play with him. Could I keep him? Please, Baba? Could he be mine?"

Niki's father put his hands on her shoulders and looked straight at her. "I know it is exciting to see a newborn donkey, Niki. And I am happy that you want to take care of him. But two donkeys are enough for one family. When he is old enough to go, I'm afraid we will have to sell him."

Niki took good care of the little donkey. She brought him water, she brought him food, and the little donkey trotted after Niki, everywhere she went. The two were great friends.

But as the weeks passed, Niki knew that soon her father would have to sell the little donkey, and she grew more and more worried.

Finally she decided to talk to her grandmother. Maybe Yaiya Maria
would have an idea, thought Niki.

Yaiya Maria was snapping beans. Niki sat down to help her. "I really want to keep that little donkey," Niki said. "What do you think I should do, Yaiya?"

"Hmm . . ." said Yaiya Maria, thinking aloud. "If your father wants to sell the donkey, then it will have to be sold. Your baba can see how much you love the donkey, and that has not changed his mind. . . . But wait—I have an idea!"

The very next day, when Yaiya Maria cleaned the house, Niki helped make the beds. Then she swept the floor and washed the dishes. Yaiya Maria gave Niki a couple of coins for her help.

Soon Niki had no time left to play. She had to work like a grownup and earn money. It was all part of Yaiya's plan.

Once a week the bird seller came to the village. Niki ran to him and asked, "Could I help you? I need to earn some money."

The bird seller smiled and told Niki she could help unload. Then, when all the bird cages were out of the wagon, Niki and her friends watched the birds for him. The bird seller gave each of the children a coin.

Niki also helped her uncle Jorgos. He had a café, and in the summertime there were always lots of tourists on the island. Uncle Jorgos had his hands full. Niki washed off the tables and brought people glasses of water and baskets of bread.

Often Niki got a few coins for a tip. She showed them proudly to her uncle. Once he asked why she would rather work than play with the other children.

Niki just said, "That's a secret!"

One evening Niki's father said, "Tomorrow is the day we sell the little donkey."

Niki jumped up and ran to the stable to be with the donkey. This was so soon! What if she didn't have enough money yet? Her eyes were blurred from crying.

Niki and the little donkey ran through the whole village. They ran until the tears dried on Niki's cheeks. When they got back home, she wrapped her arms around the donkey's neck and whispered, "Let's just hope that Yaiya's plan will work."

The next morning Niki went early to the market with her grandmother. They set up Yaiya Maria's vegetable stand.

When Niki saw her father coming with the little donkey, she quickly hid behind Yaiya, hoping to surprise him. He took the donkey to where the animals were being sold.

Niki couldn't wait any longer. She ran up to her father. "Baba, Baba! I want to buy the donkey myself! I have been working. Just look!" she cried breathlessly, and she handed him all her hard-earned money. "Is it enough?"

Her father was truly surprised. He looked at Niki with wide eyes and a smile. "So that's why I haven't seen you out playing," he said. "Well, I guess the little donkey belongs to you now, my girl!"

Together they walked back to their village. It was the hottest time of the day, and the road was long, but Niki felt like a bird.

Leading her little donkey on his rope, Niki sang the whole way home. She was happier than she had ever been in her whole life.